WHO HAS SEEN THE WIND?

Who has seen the wind?
  Neither I nor you:
But when the leaves hang trembling,
  The wind is passing through.

Who has seen the wind?
  Neither you nor I:
But when the trees bow down their heads,
  The wind is passing by.

Christina Georgina Rossetti
[1830–1894]

To the three Lauras

First Edition
Published by Henry Holt and Company, Inc.,
115 West 18th Street, New York, New York 10011.
Published in Canada by Fitzhenry & Whiteside Limited,
195 Allstate Parkway, Markham, Ontario L3R 4T8.

Library of Congress Cataloging-in-Publication Data
Harness, Cheryl.
The windchild / Cheryl Harness.
Summary: When Tom accidentally fells with an arrow a girl who
turns out to be the Windchild, the wind ceases to blow in the
village of Finn.
ISBN 0-8050-0558-7
[1. Winds—Fiction.]   I. Title.
PZ7.H2277Wi   1991
[E]—dc20   90-46372

Printed in the United States of America
on acid-free paper. ⊗

1 3 5 7 9 10 8 6 4 2

THE
WINDCHILD

Cheryl Harness

Henry Holt and Company · New York

he windmills of Finn turned to pump water for the villagers and their animals and gardens. The mills ground grain into flour for bread and cakes. The same wind that turned the mills blew the fishermen's boats out to the deepest sea, where the fattest fish swam.

On most afternoons, after helping in his father's pottery, Tom would climb the steep hill beyond Finn to practice with his bow and arrows. A gnarled and wind-bent tree held his target, but sometimes he would aim straight into the roofless sky.

One summer day Tom shot his favorite arrow into the heavens, to see how high it would go. Watching the small dark speck as it soared deep into the sky, he was proud of his strength.

As the arrow began to fall, Tom went to retrieve it. He followed it down the hill to the small trees that grew beside the stream. There he found a girl who seemed to be sleeping, but the arrow was in her side.

Gently he picked the girl up and carried her to the village, where he was met by his sister, Gwyn.

"What happened? Who is that?" Gwyn called to him.

"I don't know!" Tom looked as if he would cry. "I found her by the big hill," he said softly. "She's hurt."

"The old woman will know what to do," Gwyn replied. "We must take the girl to her."

While they hurried down the path, the girl slept in Tom's arms. She weighed almost nothing and her wound did not bleed.

At the edge of the village at the edge of the sea, the boy and his sister found the old woman, who was known as Laurel, tending her goats. She looked at Gwyn and the frightened boy and the girl sleeping in his arms. Saying nothing, she walked into her house, and the children followed.

"Lay the girl down on the bed," she said in a voice much younger than her face, which looked as old, to Tom, as the hilltop tree. She felt the girl's cheek for fever and her fingers for chill. Then she leaned down and tenderly blew a lock of the girl's dark hair from her forehead. Tom and Gwyn looked at Laurel in surprise. From the porch the windchimes tinkled, but in the garden the air seemed deathly still. The old woman smiled and whispered softly to herself, "The Windchild has come again."

Turning to the children, she said, "The girl has no fever. Do not worry. She will soon be well and strong again." Then softly she began to sing:

> *"Down to the green world dances the air;*
> *Back to the sky on the unseen stair.*
> *There live the Cloud King and his Queen so fair!"*

She sang as she made a bandage of cloth and herbs and covered the girl with soft quilts. As she worked and the girl slept, the air outside seemed to grow heavier and heavier. Not a leaf stirred in the trees, and not a cloud moved in the sky. Finally the old woman sat down heavily in her chair and the cats jumped up to her lap. The black-and-white dog lay down at her feet and rested his chin on his paws with a sigh.

After a while the girl awakened.

"What is this place?" she groaned. "I feel so heavy."

In an instant Tom was at her side.

"This is the village of Finn," he whispered to her, "and I am Tom. What is your name?"

"Thea," she said breathlessly, and fell back asleep.

"I think she'll sleep until morning," Laurel said as she rose from her chair and scattered the cats in different directions. "Your folks will be wondering where you are, children. It's time to go now, but you may come back tomorrow."

Tom and Gwyn went out into the still twilight, which was filled
with the scent of Laurel's herbs and midsummer flowers. The goats
nuzzled their hands. Tom knew that Thea would be safe in this calm
place and he was glad, but he couldn't stop thinking about her.

As they walked toward home, the evening air felt warm and close in the narrow streets. There was no fresh breeze from the sea and the sea itself was like polished glass. Usually the trees and windmills of Finn creaked and groaned in the cooling wind. Tonight they stood black and silent against the sky. In the tree branches the birds talked among themselves but sang no evening songs.

When they finally saw the lights of home, Tom and Gwyn could hear the horse whickering restlessly and the cow lowing in the stable. Father was closing the door to the pottery and wiping his clay-dusty hands on his leather apron.

"Here you are now, Tom! We'll have to hurry with the chores and milking," he grumbled.

Then he lifted Gwyn up in his arms.

"And you, Pumpkin!" he said. "Likely off visiting that crazy old woman again. Go in now and help your mother."

When Tom and his father came into the lamplit kitchen, Mother was setting out supper. She gave them each a kiss.

"Heavens! I cannot draw a breath tonight!" she sighed.

"I hope there's a storm brewing," their father responded. "We could sure use some rain."

But the next day no storm came, and the air was hot and stifling. Tom and Gwyn quickly finished their chores and trudged through the midday heat to Laurel's cottage. Thea was sitting in a shady hammock. She and Tom began talking at once. Whenever she laughed, the leaves rustled in the trees and the air felt fresh and light.

Later, when the time came to leave, Tom and Gwyn did not want to part from their mysterious new friend and Laurel's cool garden. They promised to return the next day.

After that day they came for a visit every afternoon, and every afternoon the four friends laughed and talked for hours. Thea wanted to know all about life in the village. As she grew stronger, Tom taught her games to play. She loved to run and laugh while the dog and the cats slept in the shade nearby.

Gwyn and Laurel were content to tend the garden. One day Gwyn asked, "Will Thea stay with us forever?"

"No, child," Laurel replied. "But I think she will stay for a while longer." Saying no more about it, she looked up at the empty sky and frowned. "It's sure we'll lose these peppers if we don't get some rain."

Each day the sky above was bright and still. There were no rains to cool the hot, quiet afternoons. No windy, noisy thunderstorms came in the night. The fishermen sat and mended their nets and smoked their pipes, for they could not sail their boats on the windless sea. People squinted uneasily into the unchanging blue and gathered together on the top of the big hill.

"The wind has stopped," said the miller, wiping his sweating face. "Without the wind to turn the mills, I cannot grind grain into flour."

"Without flour, I cannot bake bread," said the baker.

"And without bread, I cannot feed my children," said a woman as she rocked her baby in her arms. "This will be a hungry winter for all of us."

The Finners' voices grew louder and louder. They fanned their hot faces and their eyes searched the sky for clouds. No one knew what to do.

Tom and Gwyn slipped through the crowd and ran down the path to Laurel's cottage, where Thea was feeding the chickens. "All the villagers are worried and they've gathered on the big hill," the two children exclaimed.

"The weather will change," Thea replied calmly. "I feel it in my bones." She winked at Laurel and hugged the black-and-white dog. "Let's play tag! Tom, you're *It*," she said, laughing. Then she ran lightly up the hill.

Later that afternoon they ate blackberry pie and talked together in Laurel's kitchen. Tom told Thea's favorite tales about the fishermen of the village. Gwyn talked about their father's pots and their mother's singing and cooking. Laurel rocked in her chair and told them about her animals and gardens.

Thea told them about countries on the other side of the blue-green earth and about animals they had never imagined. Her eyes flashed fiercely as she spoke of cyclones and hurricanes, and as she talked, she seemed to be gathering strength. Tom wondered if he was fooled by the late-afternoon light—for Thea seemed to be growing fainter— but somehow he knew his eyes did not deceive him.

"Can you and Gwyn come back tonight after your parents have gone to sleep?" Thea asked, interrupting his thoughts.

Gwyn's eyes opened wide and she looked at Tom. He nodded. "But only if Mama and Papa are sound asleep," he said.

That night the children went to bed early and pretended to be sleeping. Their mother and father sat on the porch, watching the sky and talking in low, worried voices. Finally, after they had gone to bed and the house was completely still, Tom and Gwyn let themselves out the back door. When they arrived at the cottage, Thea was waiting outside.

Soon the children were running to the top of the big hill. Thea raced ahead, a pale laughing shadow, while Laurel followed, leaning on her carved walking stick. The sleepy black-and-white dog padded softly beside her.

At the top of the hill, they watched the last lamps of Finn go out, one by one. Far beyond, at the edge of the calm sea, they saw huge clouds in which lightning flashed and thunder rumbled. Far above, the full moon shone down, making wild shadows with the wind-bent tree. Down in the village, the broad-faced miller sat up in his bed, startled from sleep by the sudden creaking of his windmill.

Thea stared at the stormy horizon. "Windchild," Tom said shyly, for now he knew who she was. "I know you are leaving."

"Yes," she sighed. "I used to watch you flying your kites and playing games with the other children. I wanted to play too. So one day when I saw you shooting your arrows, I flew down low to the earth to watch. It was your arrow that brought me here—and now I want to stay. But your village needs my cooling breezes and storms that bring the rain, and I must go back to my home in the sky."

As she spoke, Thea seemed to be fading before their eyes. "Remember! The sky is more than air and stars! I will watch over you," she cried. Then she ran from them and disappeared into the sky.

"Good-bye!" they called out. "Good-bye."

Tom scrambled up into the wind-bent tree. He watched the clouds advance across the sea and felt the wind blow cool and strong against his cheek. Rain poured onto the parched fields, and the black-and-white dog barked and barked.

It was still raining in the early morning when Tom and Gwyn
left Laurel's cottage and ran down the path leading to their home.
"Wake up!" they called to their sleeping parents. "The wind has
brought the rain! The wind has brought the rain!"

All over the world the windmills turned and flags snapped and
fluttered. Ships moved on the oceans, with their sails full of wind.
In some places there were furious storms, but in the village of Finn,
the wind was always gentle.